Is Mrs. Otis really leaving?

"Shhh!" Caroline Pearce hissed. "Be quiet, everybody. I have something to tell you."

"Is this about Mrs. Otis?" I asked nervously.

Everyone turned to look at Caroline.

"Is she really leaving?" Todd asked.

Caroline nodded. "My parents drove past Mrs. Otis's house yesterday. And there's a big Sold sign in the front yard!"

Bantam Books in the SWEET VALLEY KIDS series

#1	SURPRISE! SURPRISE!	#36	ELIZABETH'S VIDEO FEVER
#2	RUNAWAY HAMSTER	#37	THE BIG RACE
#3	THE TWINS' MYSTERY TEACHER	#38	GOOD-BYE, EVA?
#4	ELIZABETH'S VALENTINE	#39	ELLEN IS HOME ALONE
#5	JESSICA'S CAT TRICK	#40	ROBIN IN THE MIDDLE
#6	LILA'S SECRET	#41	THE MISSING TEA SET
#7	JESSICA'S BIG MISTAKE	#42	JESSICA'S MONSTER NIGHTMARE
#8	JESSICA'S ZOO ADVENTURE	#43	JESSICA GETS SPOOKED
#9	ELIZABETH'S SUPER-SELLING LEMONADE	#44	THE TWINS' BIG POW-WOW
#10	THE TWINS AND THE WILD WEST	#45	ELIZABETH'S PIANO LESSONS
#11	CRYBABY LOIS	#46	GET THE TEACHER!
#12	SWEET VALLEY TRICK OR TREAT	#47	ELIZABETH THE TATTLETALE
#13	STARRING WINSTON EGBERT	#48	LILA'S APRIL FOOL
#14	JESSICA THE BABY-SITTER	#49	JESSICA'S MERMAID
#15	FEARLESS ELIZABETH	#50	STEVEN'S TWIN
#16	JESSICA THE TV STAR	#51	LOIS AND THE SLEEPOVER
#17	CAROLINE'S MYSTERY DOLLS	#52	JULIE THE KARATE KID
#18	BOSSY STEVEN	#53	THE MAGIC PUPPETS
#19	JESSICA AND THE JUMBO FISH	#54	STAR OF THE PARADE
#20	THE TWINS GO TO THE HOSPITAL	#55	THE JESSICA AND ELIZABETH SHOW
#21	JESSICA AND THE SPELLING-BEE SURPRISE	#56	JESSICA PLAYS CUPID
#22	SWEET VALLEY SLUMBER PARTY	#57	NO GIRLS ALLOWED
#23	LILA'S HAUNTED HOUSE PARTY	#58	LILA'S BIRTHDAY BASH
#24	COUSIN KELLY'S FAMILY SECRET	#59	JESSICA + JESSICA = TROUBLE
#25	LEFT-OUT ELIZABETH	#60	THE AMAZING JESSICA
#26	JESSICA'S SNOBBY CLUB	#61	SCAREDY-CAT ELIZABETH
#27	THE SWEET VALLEY CLEANUP TEAM	#62	THE HALLOWEEN WAR
#28	ELIZABETH MEETS HER HERO	#63	LILA'S CHRISTMAS ANGEL
#29	ANDY AND THE ALIEN	#64	ELIZABETH'S HORSEBACK ADVENTURE
#30	JESSICA'S UNBURIED TREASURE	#65	STEVEN'S BIG CRUSH
#31	ELIZABETH AND JESSICA RUN AWAY	#66	AND THE WINNER IS . . . JESSICA WAKEFIELD!
#32	LEFT BACK!	#67	THE SECRET OF FANTASY FOREST
#33	CAROLINE'S HALLOWEEN SPELL	#68	A ROLLER COASTER FOR THE TWINS!
#34	THE BEST THANKSGIVING EVER	#69	CLASS PICTURE DAY!
#35	ELIZABETH'S BROKEN ARM	#70	GOOD-BYE, MRS. OTIS

SWEET VALLEY KIDS SUPER SNOOPER EDITIONS
#1	THE CASE OF THE SECRET SANTA
#2	THE CASE OF THE MAGIC CHRISTMAS BELL
#3	THE CASE OF THE HAUNTED CAMP
#4	THE CASE OF THE CHRISTMAS THIEF
#5	THE CASE OF THE HIDDEN TREASURE
#6	THE CASE OF THE MILLION-DOLLAR DIAMONDS
#7	THE CASE OF THE ALIEN PRINCESS

SWEET VALLEY KIDS SUPER SPECIAL EDITIONS
#1	TRAPPED IN TOYLAND
#2	THE EASTER BUNNY BATTLE
#3	SAVE THE TURKEY!
#4	ELIZABETH HATCHES AN EGG

SWEET VALLEY KIDS HAIR RAISER EDITIONS
| #1 | A CURSE ON ELIZABETH |

GOOD-BYE, MRS. OTIS

Written by
Molly Mia Stewart

Created by
FRANCINE PASCAL

Illustrated by
Marcy Ramsey

BANTAM BOOKS
NEW YORK · TORONTO · LONDON · SYDNEY · AUCKLAND

RL 2, 005-008

GOOD-BYE, MRS. OTIS
A Bantam Book / May 1997

*Sweet Valley High® and Sweet Valley Kids® are
registered trademarks of Francine Pascal.*

Conceived by Francine Pascal.

*Produced by Daniel Weiss Associates, Inc.
33 West 17th Street
New York, NY 10011.*

Cover art by Wayne Alfano.

ISBN: 0-553-48336-6

Published simultaneously in the United States and Canada

*Bantam Books are published by Bantam Books, a division of Bantam
Doubleday Dell Publishing Group, Inc. Its trademark, consisting of the
words "Bantam Books" and the portrayal of a rooster, is Registered in the
U.S. Patent and Trademark Office and in other countries. Marca
Registrada. Bantam Books, 1540 Broadway, New York, New York 10036.*

PRINTED IN THE UNITED STATES OF AMERICA

OPM   0 9 8 7 6 5 4 3 2 1

To Alana Ramirez

CHAPTER 1

Rumors

"The Animal Guy is coming today," Amy Sutton told me as we walked into room 203 on Friday morning.

I smiled. "Mr. Crane? I can't wait!"

Mr. Crane comes in sometimes to teach second-grade science here at Sweet Valley Elementary School. We call him the Animal Guy because he always brings live animals with him.

"Those tadpoles he brought were so cute," Amy said.

"I know!" I exclaimed. "I loved watching them turn into frogs—"

"Yuck!" my twin sister, Jessica, interrupted.

I rolled my eyes. Jessica likes only animals that are cute and furry and don't smell.

"You two can be so weird," Jessica continued. "I bet you would kiss frogs to see if they turn into princes."

Amy groaned. "*You're* the one who likes to play princess, Jessica."

"*Princes,* Amy, not *Princess.*" Jessica snorted. "Anyway, I don't play with frogs. Or *boys* either." She gave me a weird look.

So what if one of my best friends is a boy? That's just one of the millions of things that make me different from my twin sister.

In case you don't know me, I'm Elizabeth Wakefield. Jessica and I are the only twins in the second grade at Sweet Valley Elementary. We're identical. That means we look exactly alike. We both have long blond hair with bangs and blue-green eyes.

Even though we look alike, we're different inside. Sometimes we're so different that we end up getting mad at each other. We always make up, though. That's what being a twin is all about.

We have different friends too. Amy Sutton and Todd Wilkins are my best friends, besides Jessica of course. Jessica's best friends, besides me, are Lila Fowler and Ellen Riteman.

We both love our teacher, Mrs. Otis. She's the nicest teacher in the world! But Caroline Pearce told us a big rumor last week. She said that Mrs. Otis is retiring. That means she won't be our teacher anymore!

Is Mrs. Otis really leaving? It's too

sad to think about. I'd rather think about chicken eggs.

"I hope Mr. Crane brings that chicken egg, the way he promised," I said to Amy.

"A chicken egg!" she exclaimed, clapping her hands together. "Wow! When it hatches, we'll get to see a baby chick come out of the shells!"

Jessica wrinkled her nose. "Eeew! I hope it doesn't smell as bad as your horses, Liz."

I don't actually have any horses. I just like to ride them. Jessica thinks horses stink.

Lila Fowler nudged Jessica's arm. "Look at my fingernails."

Jessica oohed and aahed over Lila's bright pink nail polish. Lila is the richest girl in Sweet

Valley. She always looks perfect. She's always bragging too. But Jessica likes her anyway.

Winston Egbert walked in wearing one blue sneaker and one green one.

"Did you put on your shoes while you were asleep?" Jim Sturbridge asked.

Winston slicked down his cowlick. "I thought I'd start a new style."

Charlie Cashman put his feet up on his desk. "I heard the Animal Guy is bringing a chicken egg today," he bellowed.

Winston hopped up and started squawking like a chicken. The other boys joined in. They bent their arms and started flapping them like chicken wings.

"This is what girls are like," Winston teased.

The boys thought they were being funny, but they only *looked* funny. We laughed at them.

"Shhh!" Caroline Pearce hissed. "Be quiet, everybody. I have something to tell you."

"Is this about Mrs. Otis?" I asked nervously.

The boys stopped squawking. The girls stopped laughing. Everyone turned to look at Caroline.

"Is she really leaving?" Todd asked.

Caroline nodded. "My parents drove past Mrs. Otis's house yesterday. And there's a big Sold sign in the front yard!"

CHAPTER 2

Good-bye, Mrs. Otis?

"Caroline, everyone, please sit down," Mrs. Otis told us as she walked into room 203. "I have an important announcement to make."

"Please don't leave, Mrs. Otis," Jessica blurted out. She put her hand up to her mouth as though she'd just spilled a big secret.

Mrs. Otis didn't say anything. She just smiled. But her smile looked kind of sad.

"Are you really retiring?" I asked.

Mrs. Otis sighed. "Well, I guess someone let the cat out of the bag."

"It wasn't me," Caroline mumbled.

Our teacher laughed. "It doesn't matter who told you. It's true. I am retiring."

"Told you so," Caroline whispered smugly.

I felt like crying. How could Mrs. Otis leave us?

Mrs. Otis dabbed at her eyes. "I know we've had a wonderful time together, kids. But remember when I told you about my baby granddaughter?"

Everyone nodded.

"Well, my husband and I are moving out to the country so I can babysit her all the time."

"That's really nice," Julie Porter sniffled.

"But when are you going?" Sandy Ferris asked.

"Next week."

We all gasped. Mrs. Otis would be gone in just a few days!

"Why so soon?" Eva Simpson asked.

"Unfortunately, we have to be out of our house so that the new people can move in."

"Who's going to be our new teacher?" Kisho Murasaki asked.

The thought of a different person behind Mrs. Otis's desk made me shiver.

"We don't know yet. The principal

will tell us in the next few days." Mrs. Otis sighed and picked up some papers. "Well, in the meantime,

9

we've got work to do. Mr. Crane will be here soon."

The class usually cheered whenever Mrs. Otis mentioned Mr. Crane. But I guess no one was feeling very cheery that morning.

"Let's start with our science crossword puzzles."

Mrs. Otis handed out the papers. Then she drew a big, fat chicken on the blackboard.

"Hey, that looks like the recess monitor," Tom McKay whispered.

"Mrs. Grimley?" Ken Matthews made a soft squawking sound. "She sounds like a chicken when she yells."

"Her hair is really weird too," Jessica murmured. "It looks like a big hill, the way she piles it on top of her head."

Charlie laughed quietly. "I think she's got rats in it."

"Or maybe spi-ders," Lila whispered.

I don't like it when people say mean things, but Mrs. Grimley really is scary. She's always yelling and making kids sit out during recess.

"Her eyes are beady, like a bat's." Winston crossed his eyes. "I bet she sleeps upside down in a cave!"

Mrs. Otis looked over her shoulder. "Is something wrong, Winston?"

Winston quickly uncrossed his eyes. "No, ma'am. Just looking at my nose."

"*Mrs. Otis, please come to the office,*" crackled a voice over the intercom.

"Elizabeth, please keep an eye on things until Mr. Crane arrives." Mrs.

Otis put down the chalk and left the room.

Jessica tapped me on the shoulder. "I hope mean Mrs. Grimley's not our new teacher," she said.

"Me too," I replied.

"I hope we get a guy," Todd Wilkins joined in. "Someone who'll play soccer with us at recess."

"That would be great," I said.

"Yuck." My twin sister rolled her eyes. "I want a model who wears pretty clothes."

"Me too," Lila added.

Todd shook his head. "I bet we'll get Mrs. Grimley."

"Hey, I've got an idea!" Jessica's eyes widened. "Let's start a petition against Mrs. Grimley. We can all sign it."

"Good idea." Amy said. Most of the other kids nodded.

"You write it, Liz," Jessica told me.

"You're good at doing grown-up stuff like that."

I thought about not doing it, but I was just as afraid of getting Mrs. Grimley as everyone else was. So I pulled out a sheet of paper and wrote *Room 203 says no to Mrs. Grimley!* at the top. Then I drew a big *X* through Mrs. Grimley's name with my red crayon. I signed my name and passed it to Jessica. She signed it and passed it to Lila. Lila signed it and passed it to Winston. He looked at it and laughed.

Just then the classroom door opened. Quick as a bunny, Winston crumpled up the paper and shoved it in his pocket.

CHAPTER 3

The Animal Guy

"Hey, kids!" Mr. Crane exclaimed. He was carrying a big clear plastic box. "I brought the incubator today. There's an egg inside. Come take a look!"

We all hurried to the front of the room.

"Ooh," Eva said.

"A real chicken egg!" Todd tapped the side of the incubator.

"It's about ready to hatch," Mr. Crane said.

"When?" I asked excitedly. I could hardly wait!

"Very soon." Mr. Crane grinned. He has a smile that belongs in a toothpaste commercial. "And you guys can watch."

"Ick." Jessica peered inside the incubator as if she expected a monster to pop out any minute.

Mr. Crane drew a baby chick on the board and pointed to its beak. "It takes several hours for an egg to hatch. You see, the baby chick has a little tooth here called an egg tooth."

Winston bared his teeth. "Do I have an egg tooth?"

"Nope." Mr. Crane ran his fingers through his dark curly hair and smiled again. He doesn't look like any teacher I've ever seen. I think he's even younger than my mom and dad. "Chicks use their egg teeth to break open the shells of their eggs. First the baby chick pecks from the inside until it cracks the shell. After that it makes a little hole. Then maybe a foot or a wing pops out."

I pictured a fluffy baby chick waving its little wing at me. It would look so cute.

"Where'd you get the egg, Mr. Crane?" Todd asked. "From the supermarket?"

Mr. Crane chuckled and set the incubator down on the project table. "No, Todd. Eggs from the supermarket don't hatch. I bought this egg from a farmer. Everyone calls him the Chicken Man."

"I wonder if Mr. Crane knows we

HI ELIZABETH

16

call him the Animal Guy," Jessica whispered.

Amy laid her hand on top of the incubator. "It feels warm."

Mr. Crane nodded. "It has to stay warm for the egg to hatch. I keep the temperature around one hundred degrees."

"Wow! That's hot!" Amy jerked her hand away.

"Not exactly," Mr. Crane said. "Remember, your body temperature is ninety-eight-point-six degrees. That's close to one hundred."

"Will the chick be born today?" I asked.

Mr. Crane scratched his chin. "Soon. An egg usually stays in the incubator twenty-one days. Today is the twentieth day."

Everyone moved in closer. We stared at the incubator quietly, just waiting for something to happen.

"When the egg begins to hatch," Mr. Crane said, "you should record the time when the shell cracks, when you first see a part of the chick, and any other changes in the egg's appearance."

"Cool," Winston said.

Mr. Crane raised a finger. "But since the egg is going to hatch sometime this weekend, one lucky kid here will get to take the incubator home and watch. Who'd like to do it?"

"Me!" "Me!" "No, me!" Everyone's hand shot into the air. I wiggled mine back and forth.

Mr. Crane studied us. "I need someone really responsible."

I waved harder. When Charlie put his hand in front of mine, I began jumping on my tiptoes.

I don't usually do stuff like that. But I really wanted to watch that egg hatch!

"Tell you what," Mr. Crane announced. "Since there are two days in the weekend and Elizabeth and Jessica are twins, they can baby-sit the egg. That is, if it's OK with their parents."

"Great!" I said.

"Yeah, great," Jessica groaned. She looked bored.

"Thank you, Mr. Crane!" I exclaimed. "I'll be a good baby-sitter. I promise."

"You won't be a baby-sitter," Winston teased. "You'll be a *chicken*-sitter."

Mr. Crane laughed. "Elizabeth, Jessica, you two should meet with me for the last hour of the day. I'll be showing all the second-graders taking home incubators how to handle them."

I was so happy! I looked around the room to see if Mrs. Otis was happy too. But Mrs. Otis wasn't there. I'd forgotten she had gone to the office.

Not seeing her smiling face in the room made me feel sad. It reminded me that in a few days she'd be gone.

CHAPTER 4

Party Planning

"Mr. Crane, did you hear about Mrs. Otis?" I asked as we walked back into room 203. We had called my mom from the office and gotten her permission to take the incubator home. Mrs. Otis had been there, talking to the principal.

"Yes, I heard," he replied. "I'm happy for Mrs. Otis, but I feel sad for you guys."

"We're really going to miss her." I could feel my lip tremble when I talked.

"I know you will." Mr. Crane gave

me a sad smile. "But I'm sure your new teacher will be just as nice."

Not if it's mean old Mrs. Grimley, I thought as I went back to my desk. Everyone else looked as though they were thinking the same thing.

The room was really quiet. I stared at the incubator and tried to cheer up, but it didn't work. Eva sniffled. Jessica and Lila slouched at their desks. Even Winston looked grumpy.

"I know," Mr. Crane said cheerfully. "Why don't you throw a surprise going-away party? I can help you put it together."

"A party?" Jessica sat up straighter, her eyes gleaming.

All the girls nodded excitedly. Even the boys perked up.

"That's a great idea," I said. I didn't want Mrs. Otis to leave, but a party would make saying goodbye a lot less sad.

Just then Mrs. Otis came to the door.

"Shhh," Eva whispered, pointing to Mrs. Otis.

"Well, that's it for today's lesson." Mr. Crane winked. "We can talk more about it later." He waved good-bye as he left.

"Let's get back to work on our science crosswords," Mrs. Otis said. But I barely heard her. My mind was spinning with party ideas. I wrote the word *party* at the top of a page in my notebook and began listing everything that needed to be done.

Food. Decorations. Cards. A good-bye banner. A present. There was so much to do!

"Psst—Jess," I whispered. "How can we plan the party?"

Jessica thought for a moment. "I know. I'll write a note."

I started working on my crossword. Jessica hid her note with her arm so no one could see what she was writing.

Jessica's a note-writing champ. She could turn pro someday.

When Jessica was finished, she passed her note to me. It read:

Let's plan Mrs. Otis's party!
Secret meeting at lunch!
Be there!

I thought it was pretty good, as far as notes go. I don't usually read or write them.

Carefully I folded the note up and handed it to Amy. She looked at it and passed it to Julie. Julie passed it to Tom. Then Tom passed it to Eva. Pretty soon almost everyone in the class had read Jessica's note.

But when Winston unfolded it, he accidentally knocked a book off his desk. *Bam!* The book hit the floor.

Mrs. Otis spun around and stared at Winston. His cheeks turned bright red. The note was still in his hands!

"Winston, is that a note?" Mrs. Otis walked toward him.

Suddenly Winston wadded up the paper and stuffed it in his mouth. He began to chew.

Mrs. Otis stopped in her tracks. Her eyes got really wide. "Winston?" She sounded amazed.

I was pretty amazed myself.

Winston chewed and chewed. I held my breath. Was he going to swallow it? I don't think I'd ever seen anyone eat paper before.

Suddenly Winston coughed. Then

he jumped up and spat a big, wet glob of paper into the trash can.

"Eeew! How gross," Ellen Riteman said.

"I guess he really messed up his crossword," Charlie joked.

Winston wiped his mouth with his sleeve, grinned, and shuffled back to his seat.

"I think you'd better get back to work," Mrs. Otis said suspiciously. "*All* of you."

We grabbed our pencils and attacked our crosswords until the lunch bell rang. Then we hurried to the cafeteria.

Most of the kids gathered at the same table—everyone except Charlie and Jerry. They ran off, whispering.

Were they up to something? I hoped it wasn't anything bad. But knowing Charlie and Jerry, it probably was.

Were they planning to ruin Mrs. Otis's party?

"OK," Jessica said, getting my attention. "What do we do?"

"I don't know," I replied. Then I saw Mr. Crane walking across the cafeteria. "Mr. Crane! Over here!" I waved.

"Hey, guys," he said after he'd walked over. "What's up?"

"We're trying to plan Mrs. Otis's party," Amy explained.

"Well, we should have it on Tuesday, before Mrs. Otis leaves." Mr. Crane clapped his hands. "OK. We can each bring something to the party. I can bring some soda and balloons."

"I'll bring a cake," Eva suggested. "My mom bakes great ones."

"Good!" Mr. Crane said.

"And I'll bring peanut butter-and-mayonnaise sandwiches," Winston offered.

27

"Yuck!" the girls chorused.

Mr. Crane laughed. "*I'll* take care of the rest of the food."

"But what about going-away presents?" I asked.

"I don't have any money," Ellen said.

"Me either," Caroline whined.

Ricky Capaldo turned his empty jeans pockets inside out. "I'm still paying for that window I broke with my slingshot."

"We could make something," Amy suggested.

"Great idea!" Mr. Crane said. "Maybe you can all get together this weekend and make something yourselves."

"I know!" I exclaimed. "Everyone can come over to our house. We can watch the chicken egg while we work."

"Sounds perfect," Mr. Crane said.

Lila tossed her brown hair. "I

think homemade presents are tacky. I'm going to buy my *own* gift. Something fancy."

"Well, you can still come if you want," I said through gritted teeth. Why does Lila have to be so snobby all the time? I knew that if we all put our heads together, we could make something really nice.

Just then the recess bell rang.

It was time to face mean Mrs. Grimley, ratty hair and all!

CHAPTER 5

Mean Mrs. Grimley

"Don't play so rough," Mrs. Grimley snapped at Lois Waller, who was swinging on the monkey bars. "You'll get your clothes dirty."

How could anyone get dirty on the monkey bars? I wondered.

Todd waved a soccer ball in front of my face. "C'mon. Let's play," he said. He dribbled the ball toward the field.

"Same teams as yesterday," I yelled, running after him.

Amy waved to me. We're the only girls in our class who play soccer.

Todd is pretty good, but Jerry was his partner. And I knew I could out-run Jerry any day.

Todd passed to Jerry. Jerry dribbled down the right side of the field. Just as I was about to block his shot, a whistle blew.

I stopped and looked at the whistle in Mrs. Grimley's mouth. As I stood there the ball went sailing past me into the goal. Jerry had kicked it in!

Jerry waved his hands in the air. "Whoo-hoo!"

I felt like screaming. It was so un-fair!

Mrs. Grimley charged over. "You kids can't play on the grass today," she growled. "It was just reseeded. You'll have to play somewhere else."

"But—" Todd began.

"Now!" Mrs. Grimley snapped. A

bee buzzed around her head, but she didn't even flinch. I wondered if it was looking for a place to nest in her huge hill of hair.

Todd, Amy, and I sulked over to the jungle gym. I climbed up and watched my twin sister jump rope with her friends.

"Julie jumped eighty-five times," Lila said. "Try to beat that, Jess."

Jessica swung the rope and jumped in perfect rhythm. I knew she could do it. She's the best rope jumper in our class.

Charlie made faces at Jessica, trying to get her to mess up.

"Seventy-nine, eighty, eighty-one . . . ," the girls chanted.

"Fourteen! Twelve! Sixty-two!" Charlie shouted.

"Eighty-five . . ."

Charlie suddenly ran over and stuck his arm in the way of the rope. Jessica stumbled and fell onto the cement.

"Ouch!" Jessica cried, rubbing her knee.

"Charlie, you jerk! You made her fall!" I jumped off the jungle gym and stomped toward him.

He clutched his stomach and laughed. "Ooh, I'm scared."

I knotted my hands into fists. "You're nothing but a big, mean bully!"

Charlie laughed harder.

"It isn't funny." I shoved him.

"Hey, cut it out!" Charlie whined.

Mrs. Grimley marched over. "Elizabeth Wakefield, stop that this minute."

"But he made Jessica hurt herself," I explained.

"Yeah," Jessica sniffled.

Mrs. Grimley knelt beside Jessica and looked at her knee. "I'll bring your sister to the nurse. Now, you and Charlie are going to sit out the rest of recess."

I crossed my arms and slumped down on the ground. I almost never get in trouble, but Mrs. Grimley makes sure every kid sits out at least once a week, no matter what. I scowled at her as she helped Jessica get up and walk toward the school entrance.

Winston bounced by them on one of the school's pogo sticks. "Hey, check me out!" he shouted.

Suddenly Winston lost his balance. The stick flew in one direction, and Winston tumbled in the other. He landed right at Mrs. Grimley's feet. A piece of crumpled paper rolled out of his pocket.

"Are you all right?" Mrs. Grimley cried. She picked up the paper ball.

"Yeah." Winston jumped up and brushed grass off his shirt.

"You shouldn't litter," Mrs. Grimley said, waving the paper ball in front of him.

Winston's eyes were huge. "I w-wasn't littering," he stammered. He tried to grab the paper from Mrs. Grimley's hand, but she held it out of his reach.

Oh, no, I said to myself. Was that what I thought it was?

Before Winston could say anything else, Mrs. Grimley began uncrumpling the paper. Winston gulped and stuffed his hands in his pockets. I put my hands over my eyes and peeped through my fingers. I was afraid to see what happened next.

Mrs. Grimley's smile faded, and her face turned pale. "What is the meaning of this?" she shouted, her voice booming across the playground. She aimed her beady eyes in my direction. "Isn't this *your* handwriting, Elizabeth?"

My skin was burning. I searched my brain for something to say, but nothing came up. Maybe my brain had fainted.

The bee buzzed around Mrs. Grimley's head again. I expected daggers to come shooting from her eyes any minute. When she squeezed the paper in her fist, I felt as if she were crumpling *me* up too.

Then I was saved by the back-to-class bell.

CHAPTER 6
The Secret Gift

"Hey, I heard that Mrs. Grimley's going to be your new teacher," Steven announced at breakfast on Saturday morning.

My heart sank. After recess the day before, Mrs. Grimley hadn't tried to punish anyone who'd signed the petition. She hadn't even yelled. She'd just given us all weird looks.

I think she did that to make us feel even worse.

"Where'd you hear about Mrs. Grimley?" Jessica asked.

"*Everyone's* talking about it."

Steven shook his head. "I heard she made all the fifth-graders skip recess yesterday because one kid talked in line."

"That's awful." My heart sank even lower. What if she *was* our new teacher? Would I make it out of second grade alive?

Steven laughed. "School isn't supposed to be fun, you know." He growled like a monster. "Meet your new teacher . . . *mean Mrs. Grimley!*"

"Steven," Mom warned, "stop trying to scare the girls."

He didn't have to try. I was already scared.

"Did the egg hatch last night?" Mom asked me.

I twirled a piece of waffle in syrup. "Nope. Not a peek—I mean, not a peck."

Mom smiled and held up a thick catalog. "Your friends from school should be here pretty soon. I'll put this craft-store catalog out on the card tables we set up in the back-yard. Maybe it'll give you ideas for Mrs. Otis's gift."

"Thanks, Mom," Jessica and I said at the same time.

"It'll be next to your poster board and your art kit."

When Mom opened the door, Caroline was standing there. She waved and fol-lowed Mom to the card tables.

Steven made a gagging noise. "I've gotta go before all your girlfriends get here. You guys make as much noise as a barnyard."

"At least we don't *smell* like a barnyard," Jessica snapped.

Ten minutes later our entire back-yard was full. Almost everyone from class showed up. Even Lila was there. Only Jerry and Charlie were missing.

That made me nervous. Maybe they really were planning to mess up our party!

Mom brought out popcorn and cookies and punch. She even set out the incubator. Then we all gathered around the craft catalog.

"What can we make for Mrs. Otis?" I wondered.

"I think we should make her a model race car," Ken said.

"What would she do with that?" Ellen asked.

Ken shrugged. "It's the only thing I know how to make."

"We could tie-dye a T-shirt for her," Jessica suggested.

Tom chuckled. "Mrs. Otis is too old to wear tie-dyed T-shirts."

"No, she's not," Jessica replied with a pout.

"How about this?" Eva said, pointing to a picture frame with buttons glued all over it. "All we need is a frame, some glue, and some buttons."

"That's so cute!" I exclaimed.

"Nah," Winston said. "We don't have a picture to put in it."

"You're right," Jim agreed.

"My T-shirt idea is still the best," Jessica insisted.

I pointed to a picture of a pretty hand-painted clay vase filled with flowers. "How about this?" I asked.

"That's nice," Julie said. "Mrs. Otis loves flowers. Remember when we gave her roses on her birthday? She looked like she was going to cry."

"One of the thorns probably stuck her thumb," Ricky joked.

"I like the vase," Eva said. "Maybe we could paint our names on it."

"Mrs. Otis would love that!" Julie exclaimed.

We took a vote, and everyone wanted to do it. Even the boys.

"But how can we get the vase?" I groaned.

"I can drive to the craft store," Mom offered. "It's just a few minutes away."

"Hmmm." I studied the catalog. "If we all put together whatever we have in our pockets, maybe we'll have enough to buy it."

Everyone began emptying their pockets on the table. Todd had three whole dollars. Lois had some lint and twigs. Tom had some change and a stick of gum. But no one seemed to care who was giving what, as long as we had enough money to buy the vase.

Mom smiled as she gathered everything together. "What a wonderful idea," she told us. "While I pick up the vase, maybe you can all work on making posters."

Everyone thanked my mom and began grabbing for markers and poster board. Everyone except Lila. She bragged, "I already got Mrs. Otis the best gift ever. And it cost fifty dollars."

The other kids stopped in their tracks and looked sadly at the table of art supplies. Even Jessica looked upset.

Fifty dollars! My stomach churned. What if Mrs. Otis liked Lila's gift better than ours?

CHAPTER 7

Chicken-sitting

While we made posters I tried to forget what Lila had said. Mrs. Otis was always so nice. I knew she would love our present.

Todd and Andy Franklin made a poster that read *Good-bye, Mrs. Otis!* in big blue letters. Julie and Lila wrote *We'll miss you!* on theirs. Eva and Sandy drew a big picture of a flower and wrote *To the best teacher ever!* next to it. Amy and I drew a big heart and wrote *We love you, Mrs. Otis!* inside.

Jessica and Winston were arguing. I

walked over and saw that Winston had drawn silly faces all over their poster. Some of the faces had red-and-green eyes and purple teeth. One was square with three eyeballs and two mouths. The last one had three ears.

"I want Mrs. Otis to remember me," Winston explained.

"How could she forget you?" Jessica exclaimed.

Just then Mom returned with the vase. It was big and square and was the color of sand. She also brought a long sheet of paper. "You can use this to make a banner," she suggested.

"Hey, I know," I announced. "Maybe we can draw squares on the banner, like a quilt. Then everyone can have their own square to draw and write in."

Jessica frowned. "I think it should have rainbows on it."

"But Winston has a good idea," I went on. "Everybody should draw something that will remind Mrs. Otis of them."

"Then I'm drawing rainbows on the banner," Jessica declared angrily. "Winston can have his dumb poster all to himself."

I wanted to pull my hair out. Why did everyone have to argue?

"Look!" Amy yelled. She was standing over by the incubator. "The egg is hatching! Part of the shell fell off."

We all darted over. Everyone

began talking at the same time.

"It's so cute," I said, grabbing a piece of poster board and a marker. I looked at my watch and wrote down the time, the way Mr. Crane had told me to.

"It's teeny," Amy said.

"There's the egg tooth—right there!" Winston pointed it out to everyone.

"The wing is peeking out of the egg!" Ellen exclaimed.

"Ugh!" Lila shivered. "It's all wet and weird-looking!"

Jessica pinched her nose. "And it smells."

"The smell isn't bad," Winston said. "I think the chick is cool."

"Eeew." Jessica rolled her eyes. "Mr. Crane said we had to move the chick when it gets dry. I'm not touching it."

"I'll do it," I told her. "But we

need to get some water now. And the cornmeal Mr. Crane gave us for food."

"I'll get the water," Amy offered.

Winston ran after her into the house. He must have asked Mom for the cornmeal because he came out carrying the open bag. Cornmeal spilled all over him. He was a white, powdery mess.

"Here, chicky, chicky," Winston said.

Todd helped me spoon a small amount of cornmeal onto a saucer. Winston squished the bag, and puffs of white powder floated all around him.

"You look like a ghost," Todd said.

Winston grinned and wiped his eyes. His face was still white with cornmeal, so it looked as if his eyes had big dark circles around them.

"Now you look like a raccoon," Ellen said.

The baby chick hopped out of its shell. It was so scrawny! It would probably fit in the palm of my hand.

"Isn't it supposed to walk right away?" Todd asked.

"I don't know," I admitted. The chick tried to stand, but it wobbled and swayed. Then it flopped down on the bottom of the incubator and stayed there.

"Is it sick?" Eva paced around in circles.

I hoped not. What if something had gone wrong? I didn't want Mr. Crane to think we were bad chicken-sitters.

"It'll be OK, Liz." Jessica squeezed my hand. "Let's paint the vase and let the chick sleep."

I nodded. But while I got the paints ready I kept watching the chick, hoping it would walk soon.

Some of the kids worked on the banner. Amy, Julie, Jessica, and I painted the whole vase pink. When that dried, we each painted our names on it in different colors. The vase was big enough to fit all of them.

I didn't even notice how quiet the yard was. After the chick hatched, everyone had stopped arguing and fussing. The banner looked beautiful. We'd made lots more pretty posters too. And the vase looked great. It wasn't shiny, like the one in the picture, but it was still really special.

I hoped Mrs. Otis would like it. And I hoped the baby chick would be all right until Monday.

CHAPTER 8
Somebunny's Missing!

"At least the chick isn't all wet and scrawny now," Jessica said on Monday morning. Lila was helping her carry the incubator into room 203. "It looked like a rat when it was born."

I looked into the cardboard box I was proudly carrying. The baby chick was hopping around inside it.

After the chick dried on Saturday, Todd and I put it in the box, the way Mr. Crane had said. We'd set a lamp over the box to keep the chick warm.

All day Sunday I checked on the chick and made notes on the poster board. Finally it had stood up and walked a little bit. The chick was all fluffy and yellow. Even Jessica thought it was cute.

"Great job, girls!" Mr. Crane exclaimed when he bounded into the classroom. He peeked into the box. "The baby's walking pretty well. You girls are good chicken-sitters."

"Everyone helped a lot." I grinned as Mr. Crane hung up the poster board with all my notes about the chick on it.

"Who gets to keep the chick now?" Jerry asked.

"Not me, unfortunately." Mr. Crane looked sad. "I live in an apartment. This baby will grow to be a full-sized chicken. Does anyone here live on a farm?"

Everyone shook their head.

"I could let it stay in my dog pen," Ken suggested.

"Your dog's huge," Charlie said. "He'd probably eat it."

"I'd ask my mom," Amy began, "but she's allergic to animals. She breaks out in hives, swells up, and looks like a tomato." She puffed out her cheeks.

Mrs. Grimley poked her head in the room. I took a deep breath. With all the excitement about Mrs. Otis's party and chicken-sitting, I'd forgotten about what had happened on Friday! But when she saw the chick in the box, she made a face and hurried away.

Lila tossed her hair. "See? We told you she's mean."

"I think she hates animals," Jerry said.

"And she doesn't like us much better," Winston added.

"That's 'cause you boys *act* like animals," Lila shot back.

Mr. Crane propped his foot on the edge of a chair. "Hey, you guys, Mrs. Grimley's not so bad."

"Yes, she is," Ken disagreed. "She's scary."

Mr. Crane smiled. "Maybe she's just feeling sad."

 "What do you mean?" I asked.

"Well, Mrs. Grimley's children are all grown up now," Mr. Crane said. "I heard she's been lonely since they moved away."

"If she's lonely, why isn't she nice?" Jessica asked.

"Some people don't always show their true feelings," Mr. Crane explained. "But I know she likes kids.

That's why she came to work here."

The class grew quiet for a minute. I thought about what he'd said. Suddenly I felt bad about starting the petition against Mrs. Grimley. I remembered the expression on her face after she'd read it, and I shivered.

Maybe we'd really hurt Mrs. Grimley's feelings.

Maybe she thought *we* were mean.

"I still don't want her to be our teacher," Todd mumbled.

"Yeah," Ellen said. "We want Mrs. Otis."

Mr. Crane cleared his throat. "Well, since Mrs. Otis will be a little late today, let's talk about tomorrow's party. How are the plans going?"

"You should see the banner we made," Jessica told him. "It's so pretty."

"And we made posters too," Ellen added.

"And a neat flower vase," Amy said.

I gasped. "Oh, no! We can't give her the vase without any flowers in it!"

Mr. Crane grinned. "Don't worry. I was planning on bringing some flowers anyway. Now I have a place to put them!"

I breathed a sigh of relief.

Lila pranced up to the front of the room. "Look at this bow I bought for Mr. Bunny. He can wear it to the party." She held up a black bow tie with silver sequins on it. It was beautiful.

"Let's see how it fits," Mr. Crane said.

I went to Mr. Bunny's cage. The cage door was open. But Mr. Bunny wasn't inside!

"He's gone!" I shouted.

"Oh, no!" Eva gasped.

"Start looking!" Winston yelled.

We checked under the desks. In the closet. Behind the bookshelves. Even underneath the book bags on the floor. But Mr. Bunny was nowhere to be found.

"I can't believe it," I cried. "Mr. Bunny is lost!"

CHAPTER 9
Winston's Wacky Idea

"We can't have a party without Mr. Bunny," Lila told Mr. Crane. "Mrs. Otis gave him to us."

"We can't tell her he's missing either," Ellen cried. "She'd be so sad."

"Don't worry, kids," Mr. Crane said. "We'll split up and find him. Ken and Ellen, go check the halls. Caroline, Winston, and Sandy, you can check the other second-grade classrooms. He can't have gotten very far."

"What about the cafeteria?" I asked.

Mr. Crane nodded. "You and your sister check there. Eva, Lois, and Amy, check all the girls' bathrooms. I'll look in the boys'."

"What about the rest of us?" Lila asked.

"Stay here in case he comes hopping back." Mr. Crane gave Lila a thumbs-up while the bunny hunters hurried out into the halls.

"Do you think he might be in the cafeteria?" Jessica asked.

"I don't know. Maybe he smelled the food."

"But we're having spaghetti today," Jessica said. "Rabbits don't eat spaghetti, do they?"

I shrugged. "I think we're having salad too. Rabbits eat salad."

We crept into the empty lunchroom.

"Here, Mr. Bunny!" Jessica whispered.

"Where are you, Mr. Bunny?" I called. I got down on my hands and crawled under one of the tables. Crumbs and milk were spilled everywhere, but there was no Mr. Bunny.

"It's gross down here," Jessica said. "I think I just stepped in some mashed-up grapes."

My palm felt something cold and sticky. It smelled like grape jelly. "Ugh!" I cried, rubbing my hand on a napkin I'd found under a chair. "Maybe we should just go talk to the cooks."

Jessica pushed a soggy pretzel out of her way and stood up. "They won't let us back there. The kitchen's off-limits."

A shriek rang out from the kitchen. Someone must have found Mr. Bunny!

Jessica and I hurried over. A cook rushed out of the kitchen waving a towel in front of her face.

"What happened?" Jessica and I asked at the same time.

The cook wiped her forehead with the towel. "I dropped a whole jar of sauce on the floor. What a mess!"

Jessica and I gave up and headed back to class. When we got there, everyone looked just as sad as we felt.

"No luck?" Mr. Crane asked.

Jessica and I shook our heads.

"What are we going to do?" I asked. My throat felt choked up. "The party's tomorrow. We can't have it without Mr. Bunny."

"We're losing Mrs. Otis, and now we've lost Mr. Bunny too," Eva sniffled.

"Don't worry, kids. I'll check everything one last time." Mr. Crane stepped out into the hallway.

"I have an idea," Winston said as soon as Mr. Crane left.

My eyes widened. What kind of goofy idea would Winston have?

"My cat, Friskie, is about the same size as Mr. Bunny," Winston told us.

Everyone stared at Winston as though he was crazy.

"So what?" Jerry asked.

Winston scratched his head. "I can bring him to school and dress him up with bunny ears. We'll pretend he's Mr. Bunny."

"But Friskie isn't even the same color as Mr. Bunny!" I argued.

"Mrs. Otis will be so excited about the party, she won't notice the difference," Caroline suggested.

"I guess you're right," I agreed.

"Plus a cat is furry, like a rabbit," Eva mentioned.

"And he's got whiskers too." Winston smiled proudly.

Everyone agreed to the idea. It was so crazy, it just might work.

CHAPTER 10

Party Time

"Shhh!" Mr. Crane held a finger to his lips as we walked into our room on Tuesday morning. "Let's keep it quiet. We don't want to ruin the surprise."

We all gasped. Our room looked beautiful! Mr. Crane must have been working for hours. He had hung up streamers and balloons everywhere. Bottles of soda and bowls of potato chips and pretzels were on the project table. A big bouquet of flowers lay in a wrapper on Mrs. Otis's desk.

I put the vase right next to the

bouquet. Mr. Crane put some water in the vase and placed the flowers in the water. "Perfect," he said.

"Where should we put the posters?" Sandy asked quietly.

"Let's hang them all around the room," Mr. Crane suggested. "I'll staple some to the bulletin board, and you all can tape them everywhere else."

For the next few minutes we hung the posters around the room. Amy and I taped our heart poster on the blackboard right behind Mrs. Otis's desk.

"The posters look terrific," Mr. Crane told us. "Great job!"

I felt bubbly inside. "It's like a real party."

"It *is* a real party!" Jessica exclaimed.

I could see her dimple when she grinned.

Todd, Ricky, and Ken taped the banner on the front of Mrs. Otis's desk. It read *Good luck, Mrs. Otis!* and had pictures drawn and signed by each of us. I had drawn a picture of Mr. Bunny. That was before he disappeared!

The drawing reminded me of Winston and his wacky idea. Where was he? I hoped he wasn't having any problems with Friskie. And I hoped the real Mr. Bunny would come back soon.

Eva walked in with a big cake. Purple and blue flowers decorated the edges. It had *Good-bye, Mrs. Otis!* written across the top in crooked pink frosting letters.

"It's beautiful," Mr. Crane said.

"My mother decorated it," Eva said proudly. "And I helped write the letters."

I smiled. The cake was perfect!

Lila walked in. Her arms were full. My mouth hung open in surprise when she placed her present right next to ours.

"You got her a flower vase too!" I cried in shock.

"Isn't it gorgeous?" Lila said, looking smug. "It's pure crystal. And the flowers are silk, so they'll last forever."

Everyone's smile disappeared. Ellen's face turned red. Eva's eyes watered. Even Mr. Crane looked concerned.

"Why didn't you tell us, Lila?" I snapped. "We would have made her something else!"

Lila flipped her hair over her shoulder. "What's the big deal? I mean, look at them. They're nothing alike."

Poor Mrs. Otis. She was getting

the same gift twice! She'd definitely like Lila's gift more. It was so pretty and expensive.

Jerry and Charlie came in. They had paper bags tucked under their arms.

"What did you bring?" Todd asked.

Jerry held his bag tightly. Charlie did the same.

Was this part of their plan to ruin the party?

Todd grabbed Charlie's bag when he wasn't looking. He pulled out a box of candy. "Look at this!" Todd shouted. "Cashman's got candy for Mrs. Otis! It's in a heart-shaped box too."

Charlie's face flamed. "Yeah, well, at least *I* didn't get her a *corsage.*"

Jerry shoved Charlie. "Hey, my mom made me bring it."

The class bullies had brought candy and flowers! I wanted to laugh out loud, but I didn't want them to get angry at me.

Suddenly we heard a loud meow. Winston wandered in with Friskie cradled in his arms.

Everyone crowded around. Mr. Crane chuckled.

Amy petted Friskie's head. "He looks silly."

Winston had put a band around Friskie's head. It had two fake bunny ears attached to it. Friskie was definitely the same size as Mr. Bunny, but he was still a wiggly, squirmy cat.

Several kids reached to pet Friskie at the same time. But Friskie arched his back and dug his claws into Winston's arm.

"Ouch! Stop it, Friskie!" Winston tried to hold him, but the cat bolted up, jumped from his arms, and headed straight for the cardboard box in the corner.

"Oh, no!" Amy cried. "He's going to eat the chick!"

"Stop him!" I shouted.

We tried to chase him. But Friskie ran a lot faster than we could!

"Cut him off," Jerry said, trying to block his path.

Friskie pounced onto a desk and flew across it while Todd protected the chick's box. Winston finally caught Friskie, but then we heard heels clicking down the hall outside.

"Mrs. Otis!" Mr. Crane whispered anxiously.

Friskie meowed and wriggled out of Winston's arms. The cat jumped at the homemade banner hanging from Mrs. Otis's desk. Then he ripped it right down the middle!

CHAPTER 11

The *Cat*-astrophe

"Oh, my goodness!" Mrs. Otis shrieked when she walked through the door.

"Surprise!" we shouted.

"You kids are so sweet." Mrs. Otis smiled and wiped tears from her eyes. "I can't believe Mr. Bunny tore your nice sign."

Giggles filled the room. Did Mrs. Otis really think Friskie was Mr. Bunny?

We hugged Mrs. Otis while Winston dove for Friskie. Some kids thrust cards into Mrs. Otis's hands.

Mr. Crane helped Charlie pin the corsage on her sweater vest.

"This is wonderful!" Mrs. Otis exclaimed when Eva handed her a slice of cake. "You really surprised me."

Winston held Friskie so that only his fake ears were showing. Each time Friskie meowed, someone started talking to Mrs. Otis to distract her.

"This cake is delicious," Mrs. Otis said as she walked around the room and looked at all the posters we had made.

"We made you a gift too," I told her. But just when I reached for the vase, Friskie escaped!

Meow! Friskie landed on Mrs. Otis's desk, slid across it, and bumped right into the two vases.

"Oh, no!" I cried.

The vases teetered. Mrs. Otis reached for them. So did I. But

Friskie's paw sent both of them flying to the floor. *Crash!* They cracked into dozens of jagged pieces.

Everyone screamed and gasped.

"Our vase is broken!" Ellen yelled.

"So is mine!" Lila cried. "Winston, I'm going to get you for this!" She looked as though she was going to pull her hair out. Especially when Friskie jumped down and tore up the silk flowers!

"I'll clean it up so no one gets cut," Mr. Crane said, rushing over with a broom and dustpan.

Everyone glared at Winston. He

snagged Friskie and cradled him in his arms, trying to calm him. One of Friskie's fake ears dangled sideways.

"What's your cat doing here?" Mrs. Otis asked. "And why is he wearing bunny ears?"

"Friskie thought it was a costume party," Winston explained.

"You know you're not supposed to bring pets—" Mrs. Otis began.

"I'm sorry your present got broken," I interrupted. I didn't want her to find out about Mr. Bunny!

Mrs. Otis turned away from Winston and sighed. "Don't worry." She picked up our class picture, which was sitting on her desk in a wooden frame. "I'll always remember each and every one of you." Mrs. Otis held our class picture close to her heart.

That gave me a great idea!

"Hey, everybody," I said boldly.

"Do you remember the picture frame Eva pointed out in the craft catalog?"

"The one with the buttons glued on it?" Eva asked.

"Yeah! It was great," Ellen said.

I pointed to the framed class picture in Mrs. Otis's hands. "Let's make that now!"

"But we don't have any buttons," Ricky complained.

Jessica came over with her bottle of glue. "It doesn't matter. We can use whatever we want."

My twin sister and I slipped our matching barrettes from our hair and glued them on the frame, right in the top corners.

Everyone quickly joined in, even Jerry and Charlie. Todd glued on his soccer pin. Eva added some Jamaican beads. Charlie glued on an eraser with a monster face drawn on it. Kisho added a paper football he'd folded. The whole time, Mrs. Otis held the frame and smiled. Her eyes were shining.

"The frame is really pretty," Lila said after she glued on her hair ribbon. "It's even nicer than my present was."

"I thought you said homemade gifts were tacky," I replied. I couldn't believe we were agreeing on something!

Lila shrugged. "Well, sometimes they are. But this one's really special. Plus it won't break so easily."

We both laughed.

"Thank you, kids," Mrs. Otis said after everyone had glued something on the frame. "This is the best present a teacher could have. And you are the best kids a teacher could wish for."

She wiped a tear from her eye and smiled. I knew she could tell we were all thinking, *You're the best teacher a kid could ever wish for.*

CHAPTER 12
Who's the New Teacher?

"**W**hat's going on in here?" Mrs. Grimley walked into room 203. I almost didn't recognize her, because she had a smile on her face! She was also petting something white and furry.

Mr. Bunny!

"Where did you find him?" Lois asked.

Mrs. Grimley chuckled. "In my storage closet. He was hiding under the jump ropes."

"Thanks, Mrs. Grimley," we all said. Maybe Mr. Crane was right.

Maybe she wasn't so bad after all!

Mrs. Grimley handed Mr. Bunny to Lila. Lila put her special sequined bow tie around his neck and put him back in his cage.

"I'll be going now," Mrs. Grimley announced.

"Wait, Mrs. Grimley," I blurted. "I'm . . . I'm really sorry about that petition. Why don't you stay for our party?"

I smiled when she smiled.

"I'd love to, Elizabeth," Mrs. Grimley replied. She patted my shoulder. Her hand felt warm and nice, not cold and slimy, the way I'd imagined.

"I think it's sweet that you tried to disguise Friskie as Mr. Bunny," Mrs. Otis said. "You're all very thoughtful. I can tell that you've all done a lot of hard work for this party."

"Mr. Crane helped a lot too," Caroline chirped.

Mrs. Otis smiled at Mr. Crane. "Well, now's the perfect time to tell you who your new teacher will be."

Her words made the cake turn sludgy in my stomach. Everyone sat on the edge of their seats. No one moved.

Mrs. Otis clapped her hands. "It's going to be Mr. Crane."

"Hooray!" everyone cheered.

"Are you still going to bring animals to class?" Amy asked.

Mr. Crane nodded.

"All right!" Charlie pumped his fist in the air.

Mr. Crane grinned and held up his hand. "I'm just as excited as you are, kids. And I have a surprise for you."

The room went quiet again. What could it be?

"Since Mrs. Otis is moving to a farm in the country, she's going to bring the baby chick with her and take care of it."

"My granddaughter will love it," Mrs. Otis said as she gave each of us a hug.

I still couldn't believe that Mrs. Otis was leaving. But I knew she'd never forget us, just as we'd never forget her.

And we were doubly lucky—because Mr. Crane was our new teacher!

"I guess he's not bad . . . for a *boy*," Jessica whispered. We both giggled.

After we cleaned up from the party,

Jessica, Lila, and I were looking at one of the *Good-bye, Mrs. Otis!* posters.

I grabbed a marker. "Let's write *Hello, Mr. Crane!* at the bottom."

Lila snatched the marker from my hand. "*I* should write it. My handwriting is a lot prettier than yours."

"Don't talk to my sister that way," Jessica said angrily.

Lila turned up her nose. "I can talk any way I want. You're not the boss of me."

Jessica turned beet red. I could practically see steam coming out of her ears. "Lila can be so mean sometimes," she whispered. "Sometimes I think I don't like her anymore."

Will Jessica look for a new best friend? Find out in Sweet Valley Kids #71, **JESSICA'S SECRET FRIEND.**

Elizabeth's Chicken-sitting Maze

Elizabeth is chicken-sitting for Mr. Crane. That means she's going to help a chicken egg hatch! You can help too.

Grab a pencil and draw a line through the maze, starting with the egg and ending with the baby chick. Can you get all the way through the maze without hitting any dead ends? Good luck!

Jessica's Wacky Letter

Jessica wants to write a letter to Mrs. Otis, but she can't find the right words! You can help her by filling in the blanks. Just fill in each blank with a word that fits the part of speech written underneath it. For example:

Noun—a person, place, or thing: teacher, friend, homeroom, school bus, party

Verb—an action: going, asking, singing, throwing, laughing

Adjective—a word that describes a noun: pretty, silly, boring, ugly, fun

Number—one, ten, five hundred

If you ask a friend for the different words without showing her or him the letter, it could turn out really funny! Try it!

Dear Mrs. Otis,

How are you? I'm _____. Today Mr. Crane
　　　　　　　　　　　adjective
brought a _____ to class for show and tell. I
　　　　　　　noun
brought a _____, and everyone thought it
　　　　　　　noun
was _____.
　　　adjective

Lila told me she got _____ new
　　　　　　　　　　　　　number
_____ s last week, but I don't believe her. I
noun
think she only got _____.
　　　　　　　　　　number

I saw the picture of your granddaughter you sent
to us. She looks really _____. She reminds
　　　　　　　　　　　　adjective
me of a _____!
　　　　noun

We miss you a lot, Mrs. Otis. Write back soon!

　　　　　　　　　　　　　　　Love,

　　　　　　　　　　　　　　　Jessica

Answer to Maze

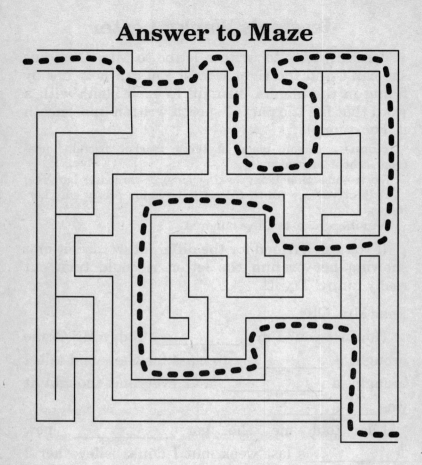

SIGN UP FOR THE SWEET VALLEY HIGH® FAN CLUB!

Hey, girls! Get all the gossip on Sweet Valley High's® most popular teenagers when you join our fantastic Fan Club! As a member, you'll get all of this really cool stuff:

- Membership Card with your own personal Fan Club ID number
- A Sweet Valley High® Secret Treasure Box
- Sweet Valley High® Stationery
- Official Fan Club Pencil (for secret note writing!)
- Three Bookmarks
- A "Members Only" Door Hanger
- Two Skeins of J. & P. Coats® Embroidery Floss with flower barrette instruction leaflet
- Two editions of *The Oracle* newsletter
- Plus exclusive Sweet Valley High® product offers, special savings, contests, and much more!

- -

Be the first to find out what Jessica & Elizabeth Wakefield are up to by joining the Sweet Valley High® Fan Club for the one-year membership fee of only $6.25 each for U.S. residents, $8.25 for Canadian residents (U.S. currency). Includes shipping & handling.

Send a check or money order (do not send cash) made payable to "Sweet Valley High® Fan Club" along with this form to:

SWEET VALLEY HIGH® FAN CLUB, BOX 3919-B, SCHAUMBURG, IL 60168-3919

NAME_____
                              (Please print clearly)

ADDRESS_____

CITY_____ STATE _____ ZIP_____
                                                                    (Required)

AGE_____ BIRTHDAY_____ /_____ /_____

Offer good while supplies last. Allow 6-8 weeks after check clearance for delivery. Addresses without ZIP codes cannot be honored. Offer good in USA & Canada only. Void where prohibited by law.
©1993 by Francine Pascal   LCI-1383-123